...for teaching me how to be the clean one.
—Christianne (Choppers)

Little Boost
is published by Picture Window Books
A Capstone Imprint
1710 Roe Crest Drive
North Mankato, Minnesota 56003
www.capstonepub.com

Library of Congress Cataloging-in-Publication Data
Jones, Christianne C.
  The messy one / by Christianne Jones ;
illustrated by Juana Martinez-Neal.
     p. cm. -- (Little boost)
  Summary: Vivienne takes pride in being messy no
matter what she is doing, but when the time comes
to clean her room she is determined to work until all
is neat and tidy.
  ISBN 978-1-4048-6651-5 (library binding)
 [1. Orderliness–Fiction. 2. Cleanliness–Fiction.
3. Determination (Personality trait)–Fiction.]
I. Martinez-Neal, Juana, ill. II. Title. III. Series.
 PZ7.J6823Mes 2011
[E]–dc22
                                        2010050940

Creative Director: Heather Kindseth
Designer: Russell Griesmer
Production Specialist: Michelle Biedscheid

Printed in the United States of America
in North Mankato, Minnesota.
062016
009823R

The Messy One

by Christianne Jones

illustrated by Juana Martinez-Neal

Vivienne was messy.

She was a **messy** eater.

She was a **messy** painter.

And of course,
she had an **extremely** messy room.

It bothered her mom.

"Vivienne!"

It bothered her dad.

"Oh, Vivienne."

It bothered her sister. **"VIVIENNE!**

Where is my favorite shirt?"

However, being **messy did NOT** bother Vivienne.

Vivienne was very proud
of being messy.

She was **so proud** that she made
a special necklace declaring this fact.

Vivienne wore her necklace **every** day.

It was her favorite accessory,
and she rarely left home without it.

But on **one** especially **messy** morning,

Vivienne could not find her special necklace.

She **searched** high.

She **searched** low.

Vivienne searched **every room** in the house!

Well, every room **except** one.

"I **can** do this!"

And with
great determination,

Vivienne started
to clean her room.

And when sweat dripped in her eyes,
did Vivienne quit?

No! She wiped that sweat away and kept cleaning.

Vivienne folded
a **mountain** of clothes.

And when that mountain tumbled on top of her,
did Vivienne quit?

No!

She picked everything up and started again.

Vivienne gathered **piles and piles** of toys.

And when she slipped on one of her little cars,
did Vivienne quit?

No! She dusted herself off and forged ahead.

After a full afternoon of
sweat, tears, and **cleaning,**

Vivienne was **finally** finished.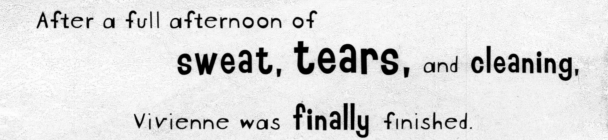

Her **entire** room was clean.

And **where** did Vivienne find her special necklace?

It was in **her jewelry box**,
right where it **belonged.**

After that day,
Vivienne changed.

She was still a **messy** eater.

She was still a **messy** painter.

But she was no longer messy
when it came to her room.

And that was
a **good** place
to start.